NED the KNITTING PIRATE

NED the KNITTING PIRATE

DIANA MURRAY   illustrated by LESLIE LAMMLE

ROARING BROOK PRESS
New York

Listen to the legend of the crew that sailed the deep
aboard a tattered pirate ship they called the *Rusty Heap*.
The pirates were a rugged lot—as fierce as they were strong.
And as they swabbed the deck one day, they sang this pirate song:

We're pirates, we're pirates, out sailing the sea.
So scruffy and scrappy and happy are we.

We're tougher than gristle and barnacle grit.
We heave, and we ho, and we swab, and we . . .

The whole crew turned and stared at Ned. The ship was deadly quiet.
"Yarrrh," said Ned. "I likes to knit. Ye might too if ye try it."
The captain stomped his wooden leg. "I won't be hearin' that!
A scurvy pirate doesn't knit, nor wear a fuzzy hat."

They sailed on to an island,

where the crew began to dig,

and when they found a treasure chest, they sang and danced a jig.

We're pirates, we're pirates, out sailing the sea.
We do what we likes, and we likes to be free.

We ain't scared of nothin', not one little bit!
We heave and we ho, and we dig and we . . .

KNIT!!!

The crew was all in stitches, but the captain's nerves were frayed.
"Yarrrrh," said Ned. "I likes to knit. This hat be custom-made!"
The captain shook his golden hook. "I won't be hearin' that!
A scurvy pirate doesn't knit, nor wear a fuzzy hat."

The pirates brought the chests aboard and counted each doubloon,
then cooked a batch of squid ink soup and sang another tune:

We're pirates, we're pirates, out sailing the sea,
as scary and hairy as any could be.
We're grouchy and slouchy. We don't ever quit!
We slurp, and we burp, and we gulp, and we . . .

The captain got so mad, he turned as red as lobster stew.

"Yarrrrh," said Ned. "I likes to knit. And that be what I do."

The captain stomped and shook his hook. "I'll not have knitting talk!

Ye'd best not knit another stitch . . . or down the plank ye'll walk!"

So Ned went sadly to his bunk and stowed his hat away.
He packed his needles, balls of yarn, and skull-trim appliqué.

He folded up his blanket with the jolly roger crest,
and stashed it with the knitted scarves, the mittens, and the rest.

That night, Ned heard a mighty SPLASH! A chill raced down his back. The captain yelled, "All hands on deck! Prepare for an attack!"

And just as Ned had feared, it was the briny ocean beast,
who loved to snack on pirate ships—his favorite floating feast.
His tentacles were thick with slime, his eyes a ghastly yellow,
and cannonballs bounced off his sides as if his skin was Jell-O.

The hungry beast ripped through the sail and gobbled down a chunk,
while Ned raced back to quarters and dragged up his knitting trunk.

The captain called, "Avast! This be no time for knitting, Ned!"
But Ned rolled out the catapult. "I've got a plan," he said.
Ned's blanket soared into the air and landed with a SLAP!

The beast was oh-so-cozy . . . he could not resist a nap.
He yawned a great big yawn and swam back down into his den.
Another hundred years would pass before he'd wake again.

The pirates danced aboard the ship and sang, "Yo ho! Hooray!
Three cheers for Ned the Knitting Pirate, hero of the day!"
And how'd the pirates fix the sail? "Knit one, purl two, repeat . . ."
The pirates knitted together till the new sail was complete.

The crew aboard the *Rusty Heap* went on about their duties,
while wearing fuzzy hats and scarves, and knitted pirate booties.
But they were still a rugged lot—as fierce as they were strong.
And every time they swabbed the deck, they sang this pirate song . . .

We're pirates, we're pirates, out sailing the sea.
We do what we likes, and we likes to be free.
We're tougher than gristle and barnacle grit.
We heave, and we ho, and we swab, and we . . .

For me hearties, Danny, Kate, and Jane
—D.M.

An ocean of gratitude to my mom, Suzanne, David,
Wayne, and my neighbor Carol Berrey
—L.L.

Text copyright © 2016 by Diana Murray
Illustrations copyright © 2016 by Leslie Lammle
Published by Roaring Brook Press
Roaring Brook Press is a division of Holtzbrinck Publishing Holdings Limited Partnership
175 Fifth Avenue, New York, New York 10010
mackids.com

Library of Congress Cataloging-in-Publication Data
Murray, Diana, author.
  Ned the knitting pirate / by Diana Murray ; illustrated by Leslie Lammle. — First edition.
    pages cm
  Summary: Ned is a pirate whose fondness for knitting annoys his captain—until one of Ned's knitted blankets saves the ship from a sea monster.
  ISBN 978-1-59643-890-3 (hardcover)
1. Pirates—Juvenile fiction.   2. Knitting—Juvenile fiction.   3. Sea monsters—Juvenile fiction.   4. Stories in rhyme. [1. Stories in rhyme. 2. Pirates—Fiction. 3. Knitting—Fiction.]   I. Lammle, Leslie, illustrator.   II. Title.
  PZ8.3.M9362Ne 2015
  [E]—dc23
                                                                                              2015013770

Our books may be purchased in bulk for promotional, educational, or business use.
Please contact your local bookseller or the Macmillan Corporate and Premium Sales Department
at (800) 221-7945 ext. 5442 or by e-mail at MacmillanSpecialMarkets@macmillan.com.

First edition 2016
Book design by Andrew Arnold
Printed in China by RR Donnelley Asia Printing Solutions Ltd., Dongguan City, Guangdong Province

1 3 5 7 9 10 8 6 4 2